Boobela and
Worm to
the Rescue

Boobela and Worm to the Rescue

Joe Friedman

Illustrated by Sam Childs

Orion
Children's Books

First published in Great Britain in 2012
by Orion Children's Books
a division of the Orion Publishing Group Ltd
Orion House
5 Upper St Martin's Lane
London WC2H 9EA
An Hachette UK company

1 3 5 7 9 8 6 4 2

A catalogue record for this book is available from
the British Library.

ISBN 978 1 84255 682 5

Printed in China

The Orion Publishing Group's policy is to use papers that are natural,
renewable and recyclable products made from wood grown in sustainable forests.
The logging and manufacturing processes are expected to conform
to the environmental regulations of the country of origin.

www.orionbooks.co.uk
www.boobela.com

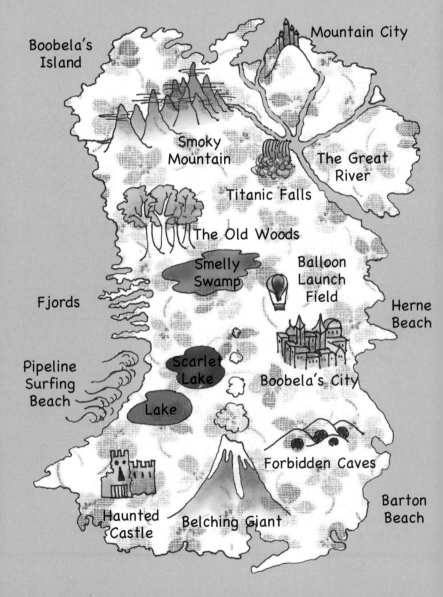

Contents

Beginnings
and Endings

Boobela stopped suddenly. Should she turn right or left to get back to her room?

Boobela had never been in a castle before. It had hundreds of rooms and dozens of hallways. It belonged to her friends, Charles and Helen. When she first met them, they were living with their two sons in a swamp. It was one of her magic dreams that had helped them return home!

Charles came out of one of the doors on her right.

"Are you looking for something?" he asked.

"My bedroom," said Boobela, embarrassed.

Charles led her there. "It's hard finding your way around, at first," he said.

"It's not just the size," Boobela replied.

Charles nodded sympathetically. "It's Worm, isn't it?"

Boobela turned away. The week before her best friend Worm had declared he was getting married to Hannah. Boobela was still in a state of shock.

"He won't forget you," said Charles softly.

That's exactly what Boobela was worried about!

"You don't think so?"

"Of course not! I still have all my friends from before Helen and I were married."

In her room, Boobela sat down heavily on the bed. She hoped Charles was right and that Worm would still find time for her. She decided to check how he was doing.

* * *

Boobela found Worm, a Smartworm, and Hannah, a Longworm, on the enormous dining-room table. They were making plans for their wedding.

"Hi," Boobela chirped. "How's it going?"

Worm groaned. "We've had to arrange separate everything because . . . you know . . ." his voice dropped.

"Longworms . . . Smartworms," Boobela completed the thought.

Worm and Hannah nodded. The two groups of worms had been at war for ages.

"Everyone will have a great time," Boobela reassured. "You two should get some sleep."

"That would be nice," said Hannah, dreamily.

* * *

Boobela lay in bed, staring at the ceiling. She had so much on her mind! It wasn't just Worm's marriage. The letter from her parents should have arrived two days earlier. It hadn't. It had never been late before.

But last month, the second page of their letter had been missing. Something was wrong.

The vivid dream came in the early morning.

Boobela was flying above a village. Somehow, she knew it was in the Dabushta Jungle. One grass hut had guards in front of it. Boobela flew down through the roof. Inside her mum and dad were sitting against the side of the hut – with their hands tied behind their backs. They were prisoners!

Boobela awoke with a jolt. Now she knew why her parents hadn't written!

She put on her extra-large dressing gown and went down to the kitchen. Hot chocolate helped her to think. On her way, she passed Worm and Hannah asleep on the dining room table. Boobela found a cloth napkin and covered them.

In the kitchen, she heated up some milk. Her parents! Hostages! What could she do?

Charles came in. "You're up early."

Boobela stirred the chocolate into her milk as she told Charles her dream.

"I need to rescue them," Boobela concluded.

"How can I help?" Charles asked.

"I'll need a very big hot air balloon and basket to travel in," Boobela said, thinking aloud. "And supplies for a long journey."

Charles stopped to think. "My dressmakers could make the hot air balloon. They've been working on your bridesmaid dress – but I think they're finished. I'll have them start work on the balloon in the morning. When do you want to leave?"

"The day after the wedding. Is that too soon?"

"They're so fond of you, I'm sure they'll work round the clock," Charles said.

"Charles," Boobela said hesitantly. "Don't mention this to Worm. I don't want him to worry."

Boobela could see Charles wasn't happy. "If you're sure . . ."

Boobela nodded. This trip would be very dangerous – she couldn't take a newly married Worm with her. It wouldn't be fair.

* * *

The next two days passed quickly. Boobela rushed around getting ready for her rescue mission. There was a lot to think about.

She'd never been further than Gran's island in a balloon. The Dabushta Jungle was thousands of miles away. It would take many days to get there. Also, she'd have to fly much higher than ever before so that her balloon could catch the fast winds far above the earth. The air would be thin and it would be very cold.

All this was frightening enough, but travelling without Worm was what really scared her. He was more than a friend, he was almost like a four leaf clover; her life had been so much better since she'd met him! She couldn't imagine what it would be like to go someplace without him.

"I never seem to see you," Worm complained as she rushed past. "You're always busy."

"I'm just getting my dress ready," Boobela told him. She crossed her fingers behind her back as she hurried on . . . but that didn't make lying to Worm feel any better. She was actually on the way to the barn where her new balloon was being made.

The dressmakers were working
in rows on one side of the barn.
"The seams need to be really strong,"
Boobela explained. "The winds will be
more than a hundred miles an hour!"

On the other side of the barn, Charles' carpenters were working on a special basket. Boobela rushed from place to place, talking and helping and giving advice.

* * *

The big day finally came. The wedding guests were due in the morning. Charles had sent two carriages, pulled by beautiful white horses, to collect Worm and Hannah's families. Boobela carried Worm and Hannah out to greet them.

Inside the first was a huge ball – of worms!

"How was your journey?" an excited Worm shouted to his family.

A terrible pong hit Boobela. What could it be?

"It was terrific!" replied Worm's father. "Halfway here, just when we got bored, the horses gave us a wonderful present!"

So that's what the smell was!

Two beautiful balloons drifted over the castle. The Balloon Club! Boobela left Worm and Hannah with their guests and ran to greet her friends as the balloons landed.

Sophie, Nurgul, Jacob and Kate had all made the trip. After a group hug, Boobela looked serious.

"Can you keep a secret?" she asked.

"Of course," they all agreed.

"I have something to show you!"

Boobela took them to the barn where her balloon had been finished the night before.

Sophie couldn't believe how big it was.

"It really is fit for a giant!" she exclaimed.

* * *

Usually, worm weddings are held under the cover of a compost bin, where birds can't feast on the bride and groom and all the guests. So all the worms were very excited about a wedding that would be held in a grand ballroom.

First, Charles' musicians played Here Comes the Bride. Then one of Charles' butlers carried Hannah down the aisle on a square of rich red velvet. Boobela, who was wearing a magnificent dress, brought Worm to the front.

The musicians fell silent. Charles, who was allowed to perform weddings in his castle, asked Hannah if she would like to marry Worm.

She whispered, "Yes."

Then he asked Worm if he wanted to marry Hannah.

Worm shouted, "You bet I do!"

Everyone laughed and Charles pronounced them man and wife. Then they kissed.

At weddings, worms usually eat as much as they can possibly stuff into their little bodies.

Charles' servants brought several wheelbarrows full of food and dumped them on a big tarpaulin in the middle of the tables. There were carrots and beans and avocados and mangos and apples – all the things worms love. But unlike normal compost food – which is old or rotten – this was fresh from Charles' gardens.

"Okay, Longworms," Hannah declared. "We want to see if you can eat more than the Smartworms. You start on this side," she said – Worm pointed with his head – "and the Smartworms will start on that side. The heaviest worm family at the end, wins!"

"Ready, get set, go!" Worm shouted. The Smartworms and Longworms descended on the mountain of food, like two huge, slow-motion grey waves.

* * *

The next few hours were difficult for Boobela. It was great to see Worm so happy and to be in the company of all her friends. And, for the first time in her life, she had a dress that fitted her perfectly and looked wonderful.

But she was worried about her parents and the lonely trip ahead, and she felt terrible that she was lying to Worm. It was hard feeling such different strong feelings.

Still, she had to smile every time she saw the two worm families climbing over and under each other as they tried to eat the mountain of food. Hannah and Worm's plan had worked – the Smartworms and Longworms were finally mixing!

* * *

Boobela was up early the next morning. She opened her curtains and saw a perfect balloon-launching day – at ground level the air was still, but high up above, the clouds were whipping along.

Jacob, Kate, Sophie and Nurgul were helping to set up the balloon when Boobela arrived. It was stretched out flat on the ground – and filled an entire field!

The Balloon Club worked as a team and the huge balloon began to fill with hot air. Soon it was tugging at its basket. It was time to go.

Boobela thanked Charles and Helen and everyone who had helped to make the balloon. Finally the Balloon Club came together for a group hug. But someone was missing.

"Where's Sophie?"
Boobela asked.

"There she is," Nurgul pointed.
Sophie was running towards them,
with Worm's travel box in her hands.

Boobela's heart sank. She had been
hoping to get away without seeing
Worm.

"What do you think you're doing?"
Worm shouted as he and Sophie got
nearer.

"I have to go rescue my parents."

"I know. *Sophie* told me."

"I'm sorry," Boobela apologized.
"I didn't want to spoil your special day."

"How did you think I'd feel when I woke up this morning and found you gone?"

Boobela hadn't thought of that. "You're married now. You have to take care of Hannah."

Hannah popped up next to Worm. "My middle name is Boadicea. I was named after a warrior queen. No one takes care of me!"

It was all going horribly wrong! "I didn't mean to upset you," Boobela said.

Worm didn't know what to do. He couldn't let Boobela go on this journey alone, but he couldn't leave Hannah either.

Hannah lent over and whispered in his ear. He shook his head. "I can't leave you. It's wrong."

"You'd hate yourself – and me – if something happened to Boobela," Hannah persisted.

"No!" Boobela said. Her bottom lip shook.

Worm saw Boobela was determined to be brave to protect him – even if it meant she was in more danger.

"Just this last time," he said, quietly, to Hannah. They kissed.

"Put me aboard," he told Sophie.

* * *

35

Worm gazed sadly at Hannah.
But as the balloon rose into the sky,
he took in all his friends and family
below. It was a grand send-off.

His thoughts turned to the
adventure ahead and he found himself
grinning in anticipation. Boobela
noticed, and began to relax.

When they could no longer see
their friends, Worm turned to Boobela.
"We're going to have a very serious
talk . . ." he said sternly.

Boobela knew she was going to get a
major telling-off. But she didn't mind –
Worm was coming with her!

Lost

Boobela was sitting huddled in the bottom of the balloon basket, wearing every piece of clothing she'd brought with her. She looked like an overstuffed scarecrow. The basket was lined with sheepskin. She was under two duvets and two blankets. But she was STILL FREEZING!

Nurgul had told Boobela that the higher the balloon went the colder it would be, but Boobela hadn't imagined temperatures like this!

Worm's travel box was next to her skin, under all her clothing. Talking to him was like chatting with someone through a metre of snow. But it was better than having a Worm-cicle!

This was their third night in the balloon. They were racing along over a huge ocean, flying high above the clouds. From her compass, Boobela could tell they were travelling in the right direction.

Because it was so cold, the gas used to heat the balloon was going fast. And they still had a long way to go.

"I've got another one," Worm shouted from beneath her clothes.

"Great!" Boobela said. They'd been telling 'warm' stories to each other.

"Once upon a time there was a planet with five suns. They kept it toasty warm, even during the night, when only two suns were on duty."

"That would be lovely," Boobela sighed.

"There were strawberries and mangoes and peaches growing everywhere," Worm continued. "And you could eat them whenever you wanted . . ."

In this way, the night passed. As the sun rose in the east, Boobela opened the peephole in the bottom of the basket.

"Worm! There's a tiny island below. We can figure out where we are!" She took off her thick gloves and unfolded their map. Worm poked his head out from a buttonhole.

"It must be that one!" he said, pointing his head at the map.

Boobela read the name. "Phoenix."

"How far do we have to go?" Worm asked.

Boobela used her long fingers to measure the distance from the island to the Dabushta Jungle.

Then she checked the scale of the map.

"We've still got over a thousand miles to travel," she sighed. She looked at the three tanks of gas they had left. They'd never make it. It would be a miracle if they even got close!

"What can we do?" Worm asked.

"Throw everything overboard," Boobela answered. "That will make the balloon lighter."

"Everything?" said Worm, thinking of his small pile of compost.

"Not our food or clothes, silly," Boobela laughed. "We're no help to my parents if we arrive frozen!"

Worm breathed a sigh of relief.

Boobela had been saving the empty tanks for the return journey, but there would be no return journey if they didn't make land. One by one they went over the side. The balloon leapt higher in the sky and Boobela turned the gas burner down to save their precious remaining fuel.

* * *

Boobela stared over the side of the balloon.

They were on their last tank of fuel, and she couldn't see the Dabushta Jungle anywhere. As she used the burner less to save fuel, the balloon started to drift towards the sea. When they got lower and warmer, Boobela threw all her extra clothes and food overboard. Every metre they flew was a metre nearer land.

The last tank spluttered empty. Boobela threw it over the side and the balloon rose for the last time.

"We're going to land in the sea," she said. She tried to sound calm so Worm wouldn't panic. "Look at this!"

She showed Worm a shape in the bottom of the basket. It was a large surfboard!

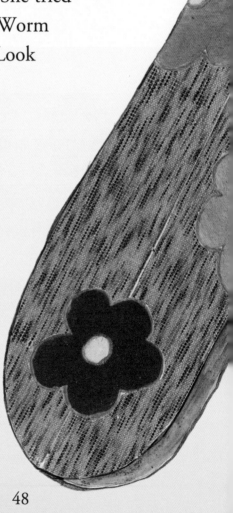

"I told
Charles'
carpenters we
might have to
land in water. Then
I told them how I'd
learned to surf, and they
made this! We'll be able
to release it when we land."

"Wow!" Worm said,
impressed.

Boobela went on. "I've got
a big, plastic freezer bag for you.
It will protect you from the water."

"You've thought of everything!"
Worm said, encouragingly. Worms are
terrified of drowning but he hid his
fear because he didn't want to worry
Boobela.

"I'll attach the bag to my back so I don't lose you," Boobela explained.

Slowly, they drifted towards the sea. Suddenly Boobela saw a bit of green in the distance – the Dabushta Jungle!

"Look!" she shouted. "We're going to make it."

The basket started clipping the waves.

"We'd better leave before the balloon collapses on us," Boobela said.

She carefully sealed Worm inside the plastic bag with some of his compost.

Then she tied it firmly to her back, as if it were a see-through rucksack.

Boobela hoisted the surfboard into the sea. Then she scrambled out of the basket and onto the board. In an instant, it floated free. They watched as the ocean flooded the basket and the balloon sank into the sea.

"Farewell, lovely balloon," said Boobela sadly. And then she started to paddle towards shore.

After a while, the tiredness from several sleepless nights hit her. She put her head on the board to rest – just for a moment.

* * *

Boobela heard a little voice from far away. "Boobela! Boobela! Wake up!"

"Go away," she muttered.

Stuck inside his bag Worm could hear the crashing of large waves. But Boobela was so exhausted nothing would wake her. What could he do? Then he had a brilliant idea.

"Pizza!" Worm shouted.

"Whaaa?" Boobela shook her head, sleepily. Her stomach rumbled. She was beginning to wake up!

"Pizza! Chocolate ice cream!" Worm shouted again.

Boobela sat up and suddenly became aware of water splashing over her legs. Then she heard the roar.

She looked ahead. The waves seemed to be breaking a long way from shore.

"I'll have to surf in," she murmured.

Boobela refilled Worm's bag with fresh air. Then she paddled towards where the waves were breaking, trying to remember everything her friend Raven, a champion surfer, had taught her.

"Wish me luck." Boobela stood and caught the wave. Perfectly. She felt a great sense of power. She tried to stay ahead of the white water and when the first wave broke, she steered into a second breaking wave.

"I've never done that before!" she thought. "Maybe I really can make it."

Then Boobela saw the reef. Just ahead, the waves were smashing into it. There was no way she could surf past that.

"Hang on,"
she said to Worm.
She waited until the
reef was almost upon
her – then she dived
off the board and over
the coral.

She hit
the water heavily –
but she had timed it perfectly and she
was over the rocks!

When she surfaced, she looked
around her. The shore was still far away.
Much further than she'd ever swum
before. Boobela thought of her parents
held prisoner in the jungle – and set off.

When she reached the shallows, she
stood, totally exhausted. The sleepless
nights, the hours of paddling, the
surfing and now her longest swim ever!

It was then that she felt something
strange. No. It was the absence of
something familiar. She reached her hand
behind her back. Worm wasn't there!

"He must have
come off when I dived in!"
Boobela cried. She scanned the water
looking for a clear plastic bag. Nothing!
She ran back and forth calling "Worm!
Worm!" But she knew even if he heard
her, she'd never hear him above the
waves . . . She fell to her knees, exhausted.

* * *

Boobela woke to find a strange, leafy shelter above her.

I don't remember making that! she thought.

"You're awake," she heard a kind voice say.

She sat up and saw a skinny man with a long blond beard sitting cross-legged in front of her.

"You've been asleep for more than twelve hours," he continued.

Suddenly Boobela remembered. She'd lost Worm!

"I have to find my friend," she cried, jumping up.

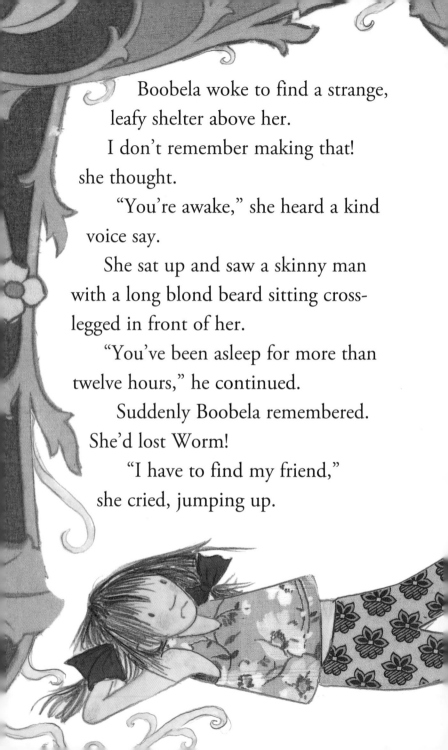

"No one else has come ashore," the man said, looking concerned. "I'm Matthew, a fellow castaway."

"I'm Boobela," she replied, hurriedly. "And my friend isn't exactly a person – he's a worm, in a clear plastic bag! I've got to look for him!"

She got up and ran to the far end of the beach, searching both the shore and the water with her eyes. When she got back to where she'd started, Matthew was waiting.

"A plastic bag would have been torn apart by the coral and the waves. I'm so sorry," he said softly.

"No!" Worm couldn't be gone, Boobela thought. What would she tell Hannah? How could she find her parents alone? How could she go on – without him?

Then she noticed that a group of birds was circling a small sandbank out in the bay.

"Look," she pointed.

"They've probably spotted something to eat," Matthew replied.

"Maybe it's Worm!"

"You'd be crazy to go out there,"
Matthew said anxiously. "The sharks
would eat you alive. You were lucky to
get to shore."

Sharks! Didn't she have enough on
her plate?

Boobela knew it would be a miracle
if Worm was alive, and that it would
be very dangerous for her to swim out
to the sandbar and back. But she also
knew she couldn't live with herself if she
didn't try. Worm was her friend.

"I have to go," she said.

Matthew nodded, recognizing her determination. "Try not to make any splashes. It attracts the sharks."

The birds were circling lower. Boobela walked into the water. She couldn't *see* any sharks . . .

She imagined her gran and her mum and dad watching over her. Then she glided into the water, doing the breaststroke, her smoothest stroke.

Boobela kept imagining she could see fins in the water, or that there was only a dead fish on the sandbar. But, finally, the sandbank was just ahead and something shiny was glinting in the middle. Could it be?

The birds were starting to land. As soon as she could stand, Boobela clapped her hands loudly, making the birds scatter.

Boobela headed towards the sparkling object she'd seen. Her heart sank. It was only wet seaweed.

But wait! The seaweed was covering something . . . Boobela tore it off and there was Worm's plastic bag!

She unzipped it and emptied the contents onto the sand. Worm looked pale and lifeless.

She was too late. Tears came to her eyes. She scooped up the sand underneath him and held Worm up to her face.

Had he moved? Or was that just the sand shifting in her fingers?

Colour began returning to Worm's body. His mouth opened then closed again. Finally he opened one eye.

"I knew you'd come," he whispered. Then his eye twinkled. "Don't leave it so late next time!"

Boobela laughed with relief. Worm was back!

* * *

"She must think you're very special," Matthew told Worm as they shared fried fish on the beach.

"I am," Worm replied. "A worm with attitude."

Matthew laughed. "I can see that."

"I wouldn't have risked my life for just a cheeky worm," Boobela smiled.

Matthew raised his half-coconut 'glass'. "To friends."

Boobela held up her half-coconut. Worm was sitting on its edge. She looked at her buddy, her eyes sparkling. "To friends."

The Ghost from the Jungle

The tide had carried Boobela and Worm's raft deep into the jungle. But now the wide Dabush river was beginning to turn. Soon it would be rushing back to the sea.

Matthew had explained that travelling up the river was the fastest way for Boobela to reach her parents. He'd helped her build the raft out of vines, reeds and branches.

It had been a wonderful journey –
Boobela and Worm had seen crocodiles,
hippopotamuses and monkeys. Now it
was time to land. Boobela leant over,
grabbed a vine, and pulled the raft to
shore.

"Well done," said Worm. He was
back on Boobela's shoulder, in a new
house made from a coconut shell.

* * *

Boobela swatted at her body. As soon as she had taken a step on land, insects had descended on her in dark clouds. And they all seemed to bite!

She was hot and sticky. Every few seconds a new vine, branch or plant hit her in the face or threatened to knock Worm's house onto the ground. She'd thought that nothing could be worse than freezing to death in a balloon, but hot, dense, insect-ridden jungle came very close!

Suddenly Boobela stopped. A plant with big yellow flowers was at the side of the path.

"I've seen this before," she said to Worm.

"Me too!" Worm agreed. "But I can't remember where."

Boobela thought. Yes! Felix and Curtis had shown her that if you crushed the flowers, the juice kept away insects.

Boobela picked some flowers and rubbed them over her face and body. She was so sweaty that the flowers stuck to her.

Magic! The insects stopped biting!

As she walked along the path,
she became aware that the jungle had
suddenly fallen silent.

Worm noticed too. "Something's
happening," he said.

Then Boobela saw them. A family
of leopards were gliding towards her on
the path. A male, a female and two cubs.
They stopped. Boobela stopped too.

She was so scared that for a moment, she considered turning and running. Then an image of Mischief, the kitten she'd befriended while visiting her gran, appeared to her. He waved his paw. "Be very still," he seemed to be saying.

Boobela slowed her breathing and let her eyes go soft.

The father leopard took a step towards her.

It was too late to run now . . . Boobela made herself be as quiet as Mischief.

The big leopard was puzzled. Most humans ran away or screamed. Then he'd chase or catch them! But this big one was different – silent, like a cat.

The leopard made his decision.
He led his family right up to Boobela
– and then passed by, brushing her leg.
She felt his damp fur, much rougher
than Mischief's.

Boobela let out a sigh of relief.

"It's strange," Worm said thoughtfully. "Everything you've learned in your adventures has helped you to survive here."

Boobela felt a thrill of excitement as she realized Worm was right! "How is that possible?" she asked.

Worm shook his head. "I don't know. It's almost as if someone has been watching over you, preparing you for this journey."

"I like that idea!" Boobela agreed.

* * *

It was almost dark before Boobela saw a break in the jungle ahead. She caught a glimpse of grass huts and she could smell food cooking.

She felt like rushing in and gobbling down any food she could find. But what if this was the village where her parents were prisoners?

Boobela backtracked and picked up a Y-shaped stick.

"Are you going to dowse to find out if your parents are here?" Worm asked.

Boobela nodded. Dowsing was a great way to get questions answered. It was the first magic her gran had taught her.

"Are my parents in this village?" she asked. The stick vibrated in her loose grip. Then the end pointed down.

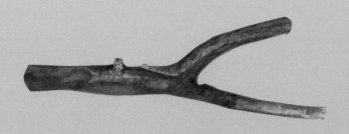

"That's a 'no'," she told Worm.

"Straight in?" he suggested.

Boobela walked directly into the clearing at the heart of the village. There was a fire there and a large, worn metal pot rested on it.

She raised her right hand in greeting, and said, "Hello, I'm Boobela."

She was used to odd reactions when she first met people – after all, nine-year-old giants are pretty rare – but even she was surprised when people ran screaming into their huts. Others threw themselves on the ground in front of her.

Not knowing what to do, she threw herself on the ground too.

Soon, people inside the huts were peeking out at her. And the people on the ground started inching away.

A pigtailed girl wearing a brightly coloured dress approached Boobela hesitantly.

"Ghost?"

Boobela suddenly realized how she must look to them – a pale-skinned giant with torn clothes and yellow flowers all over her body. No wonder people were scared of her!

She laughed and stood up. She understood the pigtailed girl didn't speak much English. And she didn't speak her language either, so she pointed to herself.

"My name's Boobela," she said. What is your name?"

"Farida," replied the girl warily.

"Could you tell everyone not to be scared?" Boobela asked, indicating the people around.

Farida smiled. She spoke rapidly. Slowly, the villagers gathered round Boobela and Worm, touching Boobela to make sure she was real.

As Boobela ate dinner surrounded by excited children, she tried to decide how to ask about her parents. She knew she could only ask once, so she wanted to do it at the best possible moment. (It was a bit like asking her mum and dad for a special Christmas present!)

Eventually, she decided that the time wasn't right. Even though the villagers were giving her dinner and a hut to sleep in – they were still suspicious of her.

* * *

The following morning, Farida and several other children woke Boobela up. They wanted to play. Boobela was torn. She wanted to enjoy a few carefree hours, but she needed to find her parents.

Worm whispered to her. "Nothing's changed from last night. You've got to win their trust before you ask."

Worm was right. Boobela decided to join the children.

Soon she was playing a game of hide-and-seek. When she was "it", it was very hard to find anyone because the jungle was so dense. But when she hid, it was easy-peasy to become "invisible". She recognized many of the jungle plants and flowers from her mum's books and her gran's lessons.

Suddenly, Farida screamed!
Everyone stopped playing and ran to
her. Abiola, her brother, was lying on
the ground. Boobela bent down and held
Abiola's wrist. His pulse was racing and
he was breaking out in big red bumps.

Abiola must have touched something he was allergic to! Boobela knew the village healer was away and she could see that none of the children knew what to do. She signed to Farida that she must run and get hot water. Then she rushed to a pega pega plant she'd noticed – she knew from her mum's books that the tops of the leaves could be made into a tea that would help Abiola.

She didn't have long – Farida's brother was already gasping for breath because his throat was so swollen. She grabbed a rock and started to smash the leaves against an empty coconut shell.

Farida arrived, breathless, carrying a coconut shell filled with hot water. Boobela mixed in the crushed leaves and started pouring the potion, drop by drop, into Abiola's mouth.

At first, his throat was so swollen it was difficult for him to swallow. But as the plant worked its magic, the swelling reduced and he was able to drink more. Soon, though still pale, Abiola was able to breathe and swallow normally again.

Together with the other children, Boobela carried Abiola back into the village. The children told their parents how Boobela had saved his life.

Farida's family approached her.

"Thank you," Farida said, translating her mother's words. "How did you know what to do?"

"I'm a healer," Boobela explained.

"We say 'shaman'," Farida replied.

Boobela thought this was a good time to mention her quest.

"Do you know of a shaman called Ralo?"

Suddenly the atmosphere changed. People's faces knotted with fear.

Farida's father spoke rapidly.

"Why do you ask?" Farida translated.

"My parents," Boobela indicated Farida's mother and father, "are prisoners." She signed being tied up.

Farida's father spoke nervously.

"My father says we can't help," Farida explained. "Ralo would punish us."

Then, as one, the villagers turned their backs on Boobela and walked away, dragging their children with them.

"A fine thanks for saving his son's life," Worm piped up, expressing exactly what Boobela was feeling.

"Did you see what happened when I mentioned Ralo's name?" Boobela asked.

Worm nodded. "But remember how scared the people were when they first saw you," he said. "I think Ralo is like a bogey man for them."

Good old Worm! He was telling her maybe Ralo wasn't as powerful as the villagers believed.

As Boobela lay down to sleep, she imagined wandering through the jungle, trying to locate her parents. "Somebody has to help me," she thought. "Otherwise I'll never find them."

The next thing she knew a cool hand was stroking her forehead. She opened her eyes. It was the middle of the night and Farida was kneeling beside her.

Farida indicated that Boobela should follow her as quietly as possible. Boobela got up as silently as she could and put on Worm's travel shell. Then she followed Farida out of the village.

When they were a good distance away, Farida pointed to herself and took Boobela's hand as if to lead her. She pointed ahead and said, "Ralo". Then Farida pointed to the sky and indicated the sun rising. She pointed to herself again. "Home."

Boobela understood that Farida would take her to Ralo's village, but that she had to return before the sun rose.

Farida used a match to light a fiery torch and led the way. Boobela could hardly see anything. Every few steps she tripped or was slapped by a branch. Sometimes both would happen at the same time – she tripped *and* got whacked. If that wasn't bad enough, the air was filled with the hoots, growls and screams of animals she couldn't identify.

Farida set a very quick pace and wouldn't let them rest at all.

"If she doesn't get back in time," Worm guessed, "the villagers will know she helped you and will warn Ralo."

Boobela didn't want the shaman to know she was coming, so she pressed on until, finally, Farida stopped.

She mouthed the word "Ralo" and closed her lips tight.

Ahead, Boobela saw a large number of huts dimly in the light of Farida's torch. Then Farida led them up a rocky path. Boobela tried to follow exactly in her footsteps, so that she didn't trip.

Then Farida stopped and pointed her torch at a dark opening hidden behind some bushes – a cave. "You can hide here."

Boobela took Farida's hand. "Thank you."

"Get rid of Ralo!" Farida said urgently. And then she disappeared into the darkness.

Boobela felt her way into the cave and found a piece of soft ground. Worn out from their journey, the friends fell into an exhausted sleep. They were closer than ever to Boobela's parents. Next, Boobela knew, she and Worm would have to figure out how to free them from Ralo . . .

Showdown

Boobela peeked through the bushes which hid the entrance of her cave. Below was Ralo's village. It was much larger than Farida's – there were at least fifty huts. But only one had guards with spears at the front and back.

She pointed. "That's where my parents are."

She settled down to keep watch. First she sat on her knees. Then her legs went to sleep so she switched to sitting cross-legged. Then back to her knees. The guards on her parents' hut were replaced by a second pair, then a third. All the while, Boobela was getting hungrier.

"All I think about," she whispered to Worm, "is my legs and my stomach. What a great hero I've turned out to be!"

Worm bumped Boobela's neck with his head.

"Silly billy. Heroes don't just charge around rescuing people. They get uncomfortable, tired and hungry – just like you."

There was movement down below. A large man with a huge horned head-dress had come out of the biggest hut. He was followed by a slim boy, about eleven years old.

"That must be Ralo!" Boobela whispered, staring at the man. "Maybe the boy is studying with him, like I am with Gran."

Ralo walked around the village as if he was in charge. Men and women looked down when he came near, and children ran to hide behind their mothers' legs.

"They're scared of him," Worm decided.

Boobela realized she was scared too.

Ralo and his assistant disappeared back into their hut.

As the sun began to set, Boobela sighed. It was going to take some time to come up with a plan to free her parents.

In the meantime, she'd have to find something to eat. She looked around. All she could see were dried-up bushes and tiny flowers.

"You can live without food for a long time," Worm told her. "But you need water every day."

She *was* more thirsty than hungry! From a torn trouser pocket, Boobela removed the plastic bag she'd used to protect Worm.

"I've got an idea," she whispered.

She laid out the bag on the bush in front of the cave. She made sure the biggest surface was like a funnel and that the bit of the bag which wasn't torn was at the bottom.

"What will that do?" Worm asked, puzzled.

"Wait and see."

* * *

In the morning, a very thirsty Boobela hurried out to her plastic bag. It was full of water!

"Where did that come from?" Worm demanded.

"It's the morning dew," Boobela replied. She picked up the bag and wet her mouth. Even though she wanted to drink all the water right away, she was careful to save plenty for later.

Then she settled down to watch her parents' hut.

"Salama."

Startled, Boobela turned to find the slim boy she had seen with Ralo standing there. He'd come up the path without her noticing! Boobela panicked. He would tell Ralo about her! She'd become a prisoner like her parents!

But the boy didn't rush away to tell Ralo and he didn't look unfriendly.

"You're Boobela, aren't you?" he asked.

Boobela was shocked. How did he know her name?

"My name is Daktari," the boy continued. "It means 'healer'."

"How do you know my name?" Boobela blurted out.

"Your mum told me," the boy answered.

Boobela was confused. "Aren't you . . . with Ralo?"

"I'm his son," the boy said gently. "One does not choose one's parents."

Boobela understood that Daktari didn't always agree with his father.

The boy bent down, so that he couldn't be seen from below. "Why are you hiding?"

"So I can figure out how to free my parents."

"I've learned much from them," Daktari said. "More than from my father. But," he glanced down at the guards, "I don't think it's possible to free them."

Daktari noticed Boobela's empty plastic bag.

"I can bring you food and water though."

Boobela smiled.

* * *

Daktari returned the following day, with food, water and two friends – Abeni, a girl, and Ayo, a boy. They were twins and, like Daktari, had been taught to speak English by Boobela's parents.

After they spent the afternoon together, Boobela asked if they would help her.

"We can keep you a secret," replied Abeni. "But we can't go against Ralo. It's beyond us."

Even though she was disappointed, Boobela smiled. Her dad always said 'it's beyond us'. He'd taught it to Abeni! It was almost as though her father was speaking through him.

After her new friends left, Boobela thought very hard. It was tough being so close to her parents but unable to see them, and she now knew everyone was too afraid of Ralo to help. It was up to her to rescue her mum and dad.

The following morning, Boobela saw all the villagers gathered together. Ralo was dressed in a dark cape and a large coloured head-dress. A thick, long snake was wrapped around his neck.

Ralo danced around chanting loudly.

Then he looked towards the heavens.
Everyone looked up. Ralo shouted and
produced a live chicken. It was as if
it had appeared through magic. The
villagers applauded wildly.

"Uncle Neill does that trick!"
Boobela whispered. "The chicken was
hidden in his cape."

Boobela was thoughtful. Stage magic
was clever and fun but it was not the

same as the magic she'd learned from Gran. Special magic came from inside you. Maybe Ralo wasn't as powerful as she'd thought . . .

Boobela took a long time to fall asleep that night. She thought about Ralo and the way people were scared of him. She remembered the time she'd been bullied on the beach. She'd discovered that bullies make you feel small and scared – and that's the only power they have . . .

Hadn't Worm said it was almost as though everything she'd learned so far was leading her to this moment?

By the time she closed her eyes, she had a plan. She didn't tell Worm. He would think it was too dangerous.

* * *

In the morning, Boobela ate the fruit
that Daktari, Ayo and Abeni had left
for her. With a determined look on her
face, she put Worm on her shoulder.
"What's up?" Worm asked.
"I'll tell you later."
Boobela marched down
the cliff path. Before
she was halfway down,
people in the village
were pointing at her,
as she'd planned.

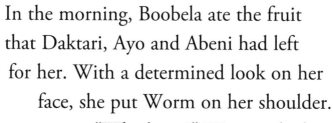

She walked straight into the clearing at the centre of the village.

"Ralo is a fake," she declared in a loud voice. "He has no real magic. And I'll prove it to you." She could hear the children translating for their parents.

A moment later, an angry Ralo appeared, followed by Daktari.

"Seize her!" he ordered.

"You see," laughed Boobela, pretending to be braver than she felt. "He's scared of me, a nine-year-old girl."

Ralo was confused. "I'm not scared of you," he said.

"You're frightened because you know I have more magic than you," Boobela told him.

"That's not true," Ralo said loudly.

Boobela smiled inside. The conversation was going exactly as she had planned.

"Prove it then! Take up my challenge. I'll sit here, in the centre of your village, the place where you're most powerful. See if you can use your magic against me. I'm so sure you're a fake, I'll happily risk my life.

If by nightfall, I'm untouched, release my parents and let us go." She knew that bullies were used to people looking away so she looked Ralo right in the eyes. "Do you agree?"

"I won't. It's ridiculous for me to test my magic against a child."

"You see!" Boobela said to the villagers. "He's a scaredy-cat!"

Ralo saw that his people were starting to believe Boobela. He couldn't refuse her challenge.

"I agree," he said. "And I'll try not to kill you even though you're a silly girl."

Boobela smiled and sat down, as if she didn't have a care in the world.

"Have you gone completely crazy?" Worm gasped. "Tell him you don't mean it!"

"I believe my magic is stronger than his," Boobela replied. "And if I don't do this, I'll never free my parents."

"But what if you're wrong?"

"Trust me," Boobela said.

Ralo came out of his hut wearing a terrifying black mask. He had his snake around his neck and he was shaking a great stick. He started to dance around Boobela, chanting and screaming.

Boobela closed her eyes so she wasn't distracted by Ralo's actions. She imagined her gran sitting next to her.

After a few minutes, Worm sniffed the air. "I can smell Gran's perfume!" he said, amazed.

Boobela felt her magic was strong. "I'm calling her. Gran would never let anyone hurt me."

Boobela could hear Ralo's chanting becoming more desperate. He was panicking because she wasn't scared. As she'd guessed, he had no power to hurt her.

After several hours, Ralo declared, "It's done!" Then he disappeared back into his hut.

Ayo and Abeni ran up to Boobela.

"You're the bravest person I've ever met!" Ayo declared.

Boobela looked Ayo straight in the eye. "You can be just as brave as me. I know it."

Ayo smiled shyly. Then Daktari came up to Boobela. He seemed to have grown older, overnight.

"My father gave me this papaya. He told me to give it to you."

Boobela gazed longingly at the luscious-looking fruit.

"But," whispered Daktari, "if I were you, I would not eat it."

Boobela understood what her friend was risking. If his father found out he had warned Boobela, he would lose his home and perhaps more . . . When no one was looking, she stuffed the fruit in her pocket.

By the time the sun was setting, everyone in the village was sitting around Boobela. They could see she was unharmed. They were losing their fear of Ralo.

He appeared again, with several of the guards from Boobela's parents' hut.

"She's a witch! Seize her," he commanded.

Ayo ran to stand in front of Boobela. "She's not!"

Abeni joined him.

Ayo was shaking but he remembered what Boobela had said. He pointed his finger at Ralo. "You're a bully and she is the only person who has ever been brave enough to stand up to you. But now I am brave too!"

The children in the village were tired of living in fear. One by one they declared, "I am brave too!" and ran to defend Boobela.

Daktari was the last. Slowly and deliberately, he left his father's side and joined the other children. He looked at his father gravely. "Boobela has won her challenge. You must release her parents."

Ralo was furious. "Seize them all. She should be dead."

Boobela pulled the fruit from her pocket. "I would be dead, if I had eaten this poisoned papaya which you sent me. I wonder how many people and animals who died from your 'magic' had really eaten poison . . ."

Ralo turned pale. The villagers realized how he had fooled them. Angrily, they turned towards him. Ralo fled into the jungle.

Boobela went straight to her parents' hut. The guards were gone. She pushed the door open.

Her parents were bound together inside. She ran to untie them.

They stood up, unsteadily, smiling broadly. Boobela pulled them close. She didn't ever want to let them go.

Her father gasped, "I can't breathe!"

Boobela hadn't realized how tightly she was hugging them!

"I heard you outside," her mum said with tears in her eyes. "I was so proud. You've grown so much." Then she added, sadly, "But you're not my little girl anymore!"

"I *never* was your *little* girl," Boobela
joked. But she knew that her mum
wasn't talking about her size.

Boobela's father noticed the shell
on Boobela's shoulder. "You must be
Worm. I'm pleased to meet you."

"Of course you are!" Worm said cheekily.

Boobela's father smiled. "Thanks for all you've done for my daughter."

"We're pals. We take care of each other," Worm replied.

"That's the way it should be," Boobela's mum agreed.

"But now," Boobela's mum and dad declared together, "we're going to come home and take care of you both."

"Does that include sleeping late, chocolate fudge sundaes and lots of candy floss?" Boobela wanted to know.

"That includes every treat known to child – and worm," Boobela's father agreed. The four of them left the hut and walked out into the village.

Daktari approached. "What will happen to us without a shaman?" he asked Boobela's parents.

Boobela's father smiled. "Your village has a shaman – you!"

"I don't know enough," Daktari protested.

"You have good judgement and a sense of what is right. And you've learned everything we can teach you," Boobela's father told him.

"And you have special magic within you," Boobela's mum added, "I've felt it!"

Boobela's father turned to the villagers. "I hope you appreciate what a wise head this young man has. He will serve you well."

The villagers cheered.

Then Ayo shouted, "We should thank our brave big friend for her help in freeing us from Ralo. We'll never be scared of him again."

Daktari nodded. He looked at the happy family. "We owe you all a great deal. But I think the biggest thanks we can give you is some time alone."

"You've read my mind," Boobela declared.

The cheers of the villagers echoed after them as the young hero and her parents walked away together. Boobela had done what she'd set out to do. She felt proud and happy. But she was also relieved she could go back to being a child again – a nine year old with parents who would take care of her.

In his travel shell on Boobela's shoulder, Worm curled up in the fresh compost he'd been given by Abeni. He couldn't wait to tell Hannah all about his adventures!